A.R. BL 1.6
Pts 0.5
F&P K

W9-BSR-727

NORMAN BRIDWELL
Clifford®
TO THE RESCUE

Scholastic Inc.
New York Toronto London Auckland Sydney
Mexico City New Delhi Hong Kong Buenos Aires

To
Daniel Jacob Morris
—N.B.

Clifford Gets a Job © 1965, 1999 by Norman Bridwell, *Clifford's Riddles* © 1974 by Norman Bridwell, *Clifford's Good Deeds* © 1975, 1985 by Norman Bridwell, *Clifford at the Circus* © 1977, 1985 by Norman Bridwell, *Clifford's Family* © 1984 by Norman Bridwell, *Clifford's Kitten* © 1984 by Norman Bridwell, *Clifford's Pals* © 1985 by Norman Bridwell, *Clifford's Birthday Party* © 1988 by Norman Bridwell, *Clifford and the Big Parade* © 1998 by Norman Bridwell. All published by Scholastic Inc.

No part of this publication may be reproduced, stored in a retrieval system, or transmitted in any form or by any means, electronic, mechanical, photocopying, recording, or otherwise, without written permission of the publisher. For information regarding permission, write to Scholastic Inc., Attention: Permissions Department, 557 Broadway, New York, NY 10012.

ISBN-13: 978-0-439-14038-6
ISBN-10: 0-439-14038-2

Compilation copyright © 2000 by Norman Bridwell.
All rights reserved. Published by Scholastic Inc. SCHOLASTIC, CARTWHEEL BOOKS, and associated logos are trademarks and/or registered trademarks of Scholastic Inc. CLIFFORD, CLIFFORD THE BIG RED DOG, and associated logos are trademarks and/or registered trademarks of Norman Bridwell.

30 29 28 27 26   9 10 11 12/0
                    Printed in the U.S.A.   23

First printing, March 2000

I'm Emily Elizabeth and this is my dog, Clifford.

Clifford likes to eat.

And he likes to play.

But most of all,
Clifford likes to help.

A kitten was in danger,

Clifford was right there.

And when Clifford's friends were trapped behind a fence . . .

Clifford came to the rescue.

Clifford's brother Nero is also very helpful.

Nero is a rescue dog at a fire station.

Clifford and I visited him.

While we were there, the alarm rang.
We followed the fire truck. Nero rushed
into the building.

Clifford helped him.

One day, Clifford and I saw a
sign that said the circus was in town.
A smaller sign said the circus needed help.

So Clifford slipped into an elephant suit
and gave them a hand. I mean, a tail.

Last year, our town celebrated its
birthday with a big parade.

Suddenly, a man ran up and stopped the parade.

There was trouble ahead at the bridge.

Clifford and I rushed off as fast as we could go.

Oh, no! The bridge had collapsed.

Clifford did some quick thinking.

Can you guess what happened then?

The big parade went on as planned,
but Clifford wasn't in it. . . .

He was under it!

One day, I was walking my big red dog
when a car came speeding past us.

And right behind it came a police car.

The police were chasing robbers.

Clifford took a short cut . . .

and caught the robbers.

The police were happy.

I'm so proud of my big red dog.

Look for the pictures from
Clifford to the Rescue
in these other funny books!

Clifford and the Big Parade

Clifford at the Circus

Clifford Gets a Job

Clifford's Birthday Party

Clifford's Family

Clifford's Good Deeds

Clifford's Kitten

Clifford's Pals

Clifford's Riddles

Happy reading!

Norman Bridwell's career got off to a big start with the publication of CLIFFORD THE BIG RED DOG. Thirty-seven years and many books later, Mr. Bridwell continues to enchant the picture-book crowd.

What makes Clifford so irresistible? Mr. Bridwell has his own theory: "I think Clifford's success is based on his not being perfect. Clifford always tries to do the right thing, but he does make mistakes."

Norman Bridwell, who was born and raised in Indiana, lives in Martha's Vineyard, Massachusetts.